Fire flies!

Story and pictures by
Julie Brinckloe

Aladdin Paperbacks

First Aladdin Paperbacks edition 1986

Copyright © 1985 by Julie Brinckloe
Aladdin Paperbacks
An imprint of Simon & Schuster Children's Publishing Division
1230 Avenue of the Americas
New York, NY 10020

Manufactured in China

48 50 49

Library of Congress Cataloging-in-Publication Data
Brinckloe, Julie
Fireflies! : story and pictures.
Summary: A young boy is proud of having caught a jar full
of fireflies, which seems to him like owning a piece of moonlight,
but as the light begins to dim he realizes he must set
the insects free or they will die.
[1. Fireflies—Fiction]   I. Title.
[PZ7.B7685Fi 1986]   [E]   85-26767
ISBN 978-0-689-71055-1

0716 SCP

To my mother and father,
with love

I would like to thank Richie Fontanez
and his friends
Deli, Frankie, Jason, Irene,
Monique, Raymond, Ralphie
and Pamela
for helping me with this book.

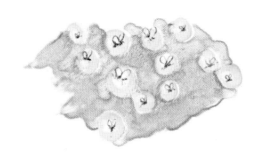

On a summer evening
I looked up from dinner,
through the open window to the backyard.

It was growing dark.
My treehouse was a black shape in the tree
and I wouldn't go up there now.

But something flickered there, a moment—
I looked, and it was gone.
It flickered again, over near the fence.
Fireflies!
"Don't let your dinner get cold," said Momma.

I forked the meat and corn and potatoes into my mouth.
"Please, may I go out? The fireflies—"
Momma smiled, and Daddy nodded.
"Go ahead," they said.

I ran from the table,
down to the cellar to find a jar.
I knew where to look, behind the stairs.

The jars were dusty, and I polished one
clean on my shirt.
Then I ran back up, two steps at a time.

"Holes," I remembered, "so they can breathe."
And as quietly as I could,
so she wouldn't catch me dulling them,
I poked holes in the top of the jar
with Momma's scissors.

The screen door banged behind me
as I ran from the house.
If someone said, "Don't slam it,"
I wasn't listening.

I called to my friends in the street,
"Fireflies!"
But they had come before me
with polished jars,
and others were coming behind.

The sky was darker now.
My ears rang with crickets, and my eyes stung from staring too long.
I blinked hard as I watched them—
Fireflies!
Blinking on, blinking off,
dipping low, soaring high above my head,
making white patterns in the dark.

We ran like crazy, barefoot in the grass.
"Catch them, catch them!" we cried, grasping at the lights.

Suddenly a voice called out above the others,
"I caught one!"
And it was my own.

I thrust my hand into the jar and spread it open.
The jar glowed like moonlight
and I held it in my hands.
I felt a tremble of joy
and shouted, "I can catch hundreds!"

Then we dashed about,
waving our hands in the air like nets,
catching two, ten—hundreds of fireflies,

thrusting them into jars,
waving our hands for more.

Then someone called from my house,
"It's time to come in, now,"
and others called from other houses
and it was over.

My friends took jars of fireflies
to different homes.

I climbed the stairs to my room
and set the jar on a table by my bed.
Momma kissed me and turned out the light.
"I caught hundreds," I said.

Daddy called from the hallway,
"See you later, alligator."
"After a while, crocodile," I called back.
"I caught hundreds of fireflies—"

In the dark
I watched the fireflies from my bed.
They blinked off
and on,
and the jar glowed like moonlight.

But it was not the same.
The fireflies beat their wings against the glass
and fell to the bottom,
and lay there.

The light in the jar turned yellow,
like a flashlight left on too long.
I tried to swallow,
but something in my throat would not go down.

And the light grew dimmer,
green,
like moonlight under water.

I shut my eyes tight and put the pillow over my head.
They were *my* fireflies.
I caught them.
They made moonlight in my jar.
But the jar was nearly dark.

I flung off the covers.
I went to the window,
opened the jar,
and aimed it at the stars.
"Fly!"

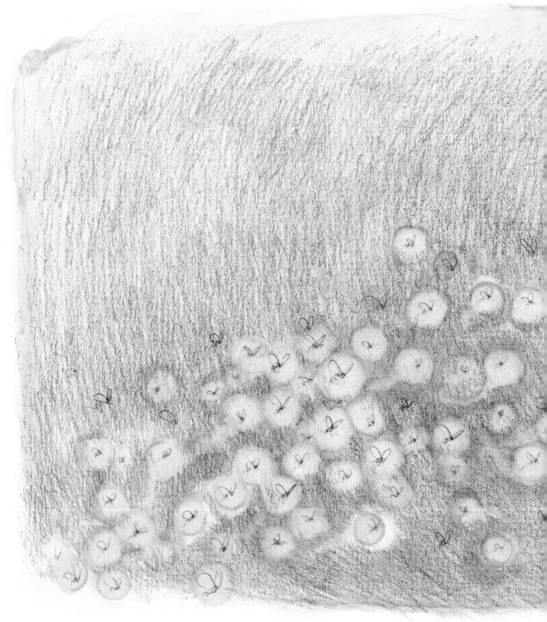

Then the jar began to glow,
green,
then gold,
then white as the moon.
And the fireflies poured out into the night.

Fireflies!
Blinking on, blinking off,
dipping low, soaring high above my head,
making circles around the moon,
like stars dancing.

I held the jar, dark and empty,
in my hands.
The moonlight and the fireflies
swam in my tears,

but I could feel myself smiling.